a small blue whale

Story by BETH FERRY   Pictures by LISA MUNDORFF

Alfred A. Knopf

New York

For Sheila and Joanne, true-blue friends —B.F.

For Merret and Harlan, with all my heart —L.M.

THIS IS A BORZOI BOOK PUBLISHED BY ALFRED A. KNOPF

Text copyright © 2017 by Beth Ferry
Jacket art and interior illustrations copyright © 2017 by Lisa Mundorff

Visit us on the Web! randomhousekids.com
Educators and librarians, for a variety of teaching tools, visit us at RHTeachersLibrarians.com

Library of Congress Cataloging-in-Publication Data is available upon request.
ISBN 978-1-5247-1337-9 (trade) — ISBN 978-1-5247-1338-6 (lib. bdg.) — ISBN 978-1-5247-1339-3 (ebook)

MANUFACTURED IN CHINA
October 2017
10 9 8 7 6 5 4 3 2 1
First Edition

A small blue whale sat in a silver sea

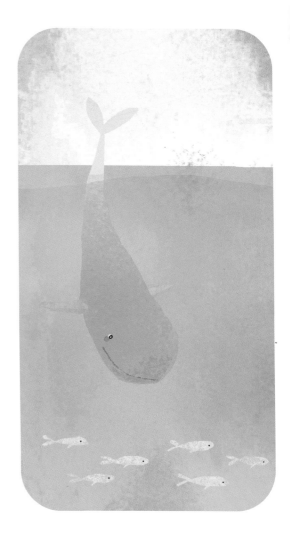

wishing,

wanting,

waiting for
a friend.

Waiting was hard, but he didn't mind;
he was sure a friend would be
worth the wait.

As the sun rose,
he glimpsed a glint of gold,
followed by an inkling of orange
and radiant ribbons of red.

The colors were so beautiful that the
whale wondered if this was what
friendship *looked* like.

The sun grew stronger. It was warm
and steady. The whale wondered if
this was what friendship *felt* like.

As he basked, he noticed
a small pink cloud.

Could this be the friend he'd been
waiting for? "Hello!" he called.

The cloud drifted across the sun and sent
down a small sprinkling of raindrops.
"I agree," the whale said.
"It is rather warm today."

As he licked the sweet, cool drops,
the whale thought that this must be
what friendship *tasted* like.

The cloud billowed away.
"Wonderful idea," the whale said.
"I've always wanted to travel south."

The whale and the cloud traveled together happily. The whale was sure this was what friends did.

They settled under a sky full of stars.
"Let's count them," the whale said.
"One, two . . ."

The cloud released one, then two,
then hundreds of raindrops.
The whale couldn't keep up.

"You're right," he laughed.
"There are too many to count."

One morning, the sun shone squarely on the
small pink cloud. A rainbow appeared.

So did a trio of bouncing penguins.

They leapt and swooped.
And laughed and whooped
as they tried to catch the colors.
The whale was sure this was what
friendship *sounded* like.

He wanted to help.
Isn't that what friends did?

He heaved himself onto the ice.
"Hop on," he called.

"*Whee!*" sang the penguins as the whale flung them high into the sky, so close to the small pink cloud, who . . .

was swirling away.
"Wait!" called the whale.
He tried to follow, but . . .

. . . he was stuck.

The penguins clicked their bills,
tapped their feet, shook their heads.

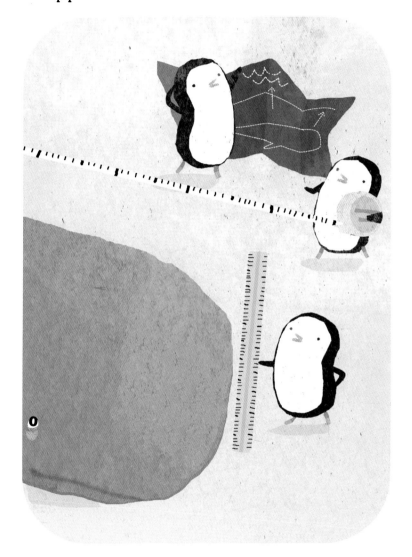

One by one, they waddled away.

A sad blue whale sat on the milky ice

wishing,

wanting,

waiting for help.

One, then two, then hundreds
of snowflakes floated down,

just as one, then two, then hundreds
of penguins appeared!

They scooped the snow, making a slippery slide.
They pushed and pushed.
Then they clambered aboard.

"*Whee!*" shouted the penguins.
"Free!" shouted the whale as he splashed into the sea.

The penguins sent up an enormous cheer.
The whale sent up a huge spray of thanks.
The clouds sent down flurries of frozen confetti.

Finally, the whale knew *exactly* what friendship

looked like,   sounded like,   tasted like,

and felt like.

And it had definitely been worth the wait.